AMISH ESCAPE

Amish Romance

HANNAH MILLER

Tica House
Publishing

Sweet Romance that Delights and Enchants!

Personal Word from the Author

To My Dear Readers,

How exciting that you have chosen one of my books to read. Thank you! I am proud to now be part of the team of writers at Tica House Publishing who work joyfully to bring you stories of hope, faith, courage, and love.

Please feel free to contact me as I love to hear from my readers. I would like to personally invite you to sign up for updates and to become part of our **Exclusive Reader Club** —it's completely Free to join! Hope to see you there!

With love,

Hannah Miller

VISIT HERE to Join our Reader's Club and to Receive Tica House Updates:

https://amish.subscribemenow.com/

Chapter One

Marlene Burki was the last passenger to step out of the stifling heat of the overcrowded bus. She waited until all the others had pushed, shoved, and grumbled their way to the doors: a gaggle of giggling teenagers with dyed hair and glittering smartphones, a man with a briefcase barking into his phone, a harassed young mother trying to wrangle three unruly children. They were all so alien to her, and so she only moved when they had all disappeared into the sweltering summery day outside. Only then did she rise, clutching a small bag nervously in her trembling white hands, holding it close against her black apron.

The bus driver gave her a curious glance when she walked forward, his eyes raking her from her plain black *kapp* to her sturdy boots, which had no laces. Marlene was grateful that he said nothing.

Stepping out at the silent bus stop at Baker's Corner, Marlene was relieved to see that most of the other passengers had already dispersed into waiting cars. She avoided them, heading to an unoccupied bench nearby. Sitting down, she kept her bag on her lap and allowed herself a deep breath. She'd survived this leg of her journey, at least. It was almost over. And so far, it didn't seem like Jeremy had followed her.

Marlene's back ached. She wanted to lean against the bench and relax, but she found herself scanning the road up and down, taking in this sleepy little corner of a mainly Amish town. Little had changed since she'd last been here. There was still the winding main street that meandered aimlessly from one shop to another, most of them almost empty, catering to the few things that the surrounding farmers couldn't produce themselves. A horse, hitched to an open-topped buggy, was tied in front of the fabric store. Apart from the growl of the departing bus, and the ringing of hammer on steel from the smithy, there was almost no noise.

The last time Marlene had left Baker's Corner hadn't been in a bus. It had been in an open-topped buggy like that one, drawn by a fine young horse that Jeremy had just purchased. She remembered, even then, being nervous about leaving her home behind. But all she wanted was to get away from a town where everyone seemed to have a family except her. With Jeremy, she could build a new family, and she'd been trying hard to cling to that dream as she held onto his arm and waved goodbye to Aunt Sarah. The horse's hooves had sounded so cheerful then as they carried her away into a future that had never turned out to be what she wanted.

She laid a hand on her belly, swallowing hard as wave of fear clutched at her. Maybe she'd been a fool to come back here. It would be the very first place he would look. But she had nowhere else to go, and she had to go somewhere – not for herself, but for the little life growing inside her.

The rattle of an oncoming buggy shook her. She jumped up, terrified to see that same fine young horse coming toward her, but instead it was the big-eared bay gelding she'd grown up with. He was jogging unhurriedly up the main street toward her with Sarah's smiling face at the other end of the reins.

"Sarah!" Marlene felt an unexpected wave of relief wash over her like warm bathwater. She hurried past the bench to where the old horse was coming to a halt.

Marlene's only surviving relative, a widow with a face as pleasantly wrinkled as a prune, lifted her creased face into a warm smile. "It's so *gut* to see you," she cried, scrambling with difficulty down from the buggy. Her embrace was wonderful: gnarled and sincere, and smelling faintly of lavender.

"It's *gut* to see you too, Sarah," said Marlene. She struggled to blink back her tears, not wanting Sarah to see them.

"What a stroke of luck for me that Jeremy's cousin had the accident and needed his help right at this minute." Sarah grinned, chuckling to herself. "Well, I'm sure the bishop wouldn't like to hear me say that, but I'm glad that you had to come and stay with me for a while at any rate." She gripped Marlene's hand, and suddenly those shrewd little dark eyes were searching Marlene's face more sharply than Marlene had expected. "Are you all right?" she said softly.

"Well – hungry," said Marlene, laughing lightly, the way she'd done a thousand times at church when her friends had asked her. "And perhaps a little moody."

"That's only natural in your condition." Sarah patted Marlene's cheek. "Come on – let's not waste time standing about here in the sun. I have lovely cold meats waiting for us back home."

The buggy rumbled off back down the street, heading out into the surrounding farmland that basked in verdant green beneath the summer sun. Marlene couldn't help glancing over her shoulder just once. It was all so peaceful here, yet she couldn't forget the threat that had driven her back home.

She prayed that she would somehow be safe here.

Birdsong trickled through the air in glittering liquid drops of sound, splashing gently on Marlene's consciousness, reviving it from her dreamless sleep. She kept her eyes closed, unmoving as she listened to the sound of the birds. She had to snatch her peace wherever she could get it. The days were so long at times on the farm with Jeremy and no one else around...

No one but the little one. Her eyes snapped open, and for an appalling moment, she was back home. But when she rolled over, her outstretched fingers met nothing but linen, and the memories rushed back to her. She was safely in Sarah's house.

It was still early, but Marlene knew that it wouldn't be long before her aunt was up, too. She made her bed with quick, neat movements, grateful for the peaceful silence of her bedroom. A beautifully carved wooden wardrobe in the opposite corner of the room was ample space for the few clothes that had fit in her little bag. She pulled a dark green dress over her head, put up her hair by feel, and tucked her *kapp* neatly over it.

Fully presentable, Marlene headed for the window beside the wardrobe and pulled the curtains wide. The view that greeted her was a familiar one, and it seemed to soothe her almost instantly. Her times spent visiting Sarah and her late uncle had been some of the best in her life; the only times when she'd felt like she belonged. And this view had always been a part of those times. Leaning her elbows on the windowsill, she gazed out at the miles of green hills crisscrossed with post-and-rail fences and sturdy old stone walls. In the golden morning light, Sarah's herd of beef cattle were bronze-bright specks on the grass. The little barn was surrounded by a happy series of clucking chickens. The bay gelding stood in his box stall, his head over the bottom door, ears pricked toward the feed room. For a childlike moment, Marlene hoped that Sarah would let her feed him and feel the silken gentleness of his muzzle searching her apron for treats.

She was about to turn away when the gelding lifted his nose and uttered a soft whinny of recognition. The feed room door opened, and a man stepped out. The moment his broad-shouldered figure appeared in the sunlight, casting a long westward shadow behind him, it was as if the sky had suddenly turned darker. His sturdy shape was an unfamiliar one, but it didn't have to be familiar to send a lance of terror through Marlene's heart. She couldn't stop herself from uttering a tiny gasp of fright as she stepped back from the window.

It was a mistake. The man stopped, turning around, his eyes scanning the farmhouse; they were hidden under the brim of his straw hat, and Marlene saw that his cheeks were clean-shaven. She yanked at the curtains, closing them again, her heart hammering. The sight of the stranger seemed to have frozen her in place as surely as if her feet had taken root in the simple wooden floor.

She only found the strength to move when she heard a gentle clank from downstairs – the unmistakable sound of Sarah putting the kettle on. Taking small, wobbly steps, Marlene stumbled down the stairs and into the large open kitchen with its rows of wooden cabinets and comfortable gas stove squatting in the corner. The copper kettle was already steaming above the blue gas flame, and Sarah stood by the counter, putting out mugs and teaspoons.

"S-Sarah?" Marlene croaked.

"Marlene," Sarah turned, beaming. "Ah, you could have had a little lie-in, you know. I was going to bring up your coffee." Her wrinkled brow furrowed even further. "*Liebchen*, you're as white as a sheet. What's the matter?"

"Who..." Marlene took a shaky breath. It felt as though the very air had been stolen from her lungs. "Who is that man outside in the yard?"

"Oh." Sarah laughed. "I'm sorry. I forgot to tell you he'd be around. That's just Zeb. He helps me with all the feeding and milking – I can't do all that with my bad hip, you know."

"Is he – all right?" Marlene croaked.

"Right as rain, my dear *maidel*. Zeb's an old family friend. Why, you two played together when you were *kinner*, although that was years ago. I don't expect you to remember."

"Oh." Marlene sank into a chair. "I don't."

"Sorry, Marlene." Sarah put a plate of chocolate chip muffins in front of her. "I didn't think to tell you. You must have thought he was a burglar of some kind."

Marlene smiled. "Silly of me, really," she said, laughing despite the fluttery feeling that still churned and roiled in her gut. "I should have known he was all right when old Muddy recognized him."

Sarah laughed. "*Jah*, Muddy's always been a *gut* judge of character," she said. "Do you remember when he kicked that farrier all the way across the smithy, and it turned out the man had been stealing chickens from farms?"

"I do," said Marlene. She also remembered a time when the old horse had snapped at Jeremy, almost taking a chunk out of his shoulder, and now she felt a pang of regret for yelling at him. Clearly, Muddy had known better than she had. But she couldn't tell any of that to Sarah.

Sarah finished up the coffee and held it out, chattering constantly about chickens and sewing and village talk, and Marlene tried her best to listen as she took the mug and sipped at the strong, fragrant fluid. Surely everything was all right, she thought, watching as Sarah started busily cracking eggs into a pan for breakfast. Sarah trusted Zeb; couldn't that be good enough?

Sarah had trusted Jeremy, too. Marlene vowed quietly to keep a very good eye on her aunt's farm hand. *Ach,* but she was becoming suspicious of everyone, and it troubled her. But she'd learned the hard way not to take anyone—especially a man—at face value.

Zebadiah Hartzler lowered the bucket of feed into the metal bracket in the corner of the old bay gelding's stall. As always, Muddy gave a grateful little snort, then plunged his face into the bucket up to the eyes and started champing at it bravely with his few remaining teeth.

"*Gut* boy," murmured Zeb, feeling a flush of quiet satisfaction as he rubbed a hand over the horse's soft neck. "There's a *gut* boy."

He paused, one elbow leaning on the stable door, and looked up over his shoulder at the window of the spare bedroom. The curtains were still closed; they hadn't stirred, and part of him wondered if he'd imagined the girl. He closed his eyes, trying to summon the memory. She'd come and gone so quickly that she could well have been little more than a vision, yet the details were etched deep in his mind: her sad eyes gazing down at the barn. Her skin was tanned sweet caramel under what he imagined would be freckles, running up to meet a hairline that flashed vivid red before disappearing under her *kapp*. Haloed by the morning light, she was something that Zeb didn't often come across: a new face. He'd grown up in Baker's Corner, and he felt at times that he knew everyone.

Everyone but this girl. She must be Sarah's niece, the one that the old lady had briefly told him would be coming over to stay. Sarah hadn't said why or for how long, but Zeb was beginning to hope that this wasn't just a weekend visit.

The front door of the farmhouse swung open, setting free a burst of delicious smells: toast, frying bacon, coffee.

"Zeb!" Sarah wheezed. "Come on in for a bite!"

"*Danke*, Sarah," called Zeb. "I'll be right there."

He hurried, his heart pounding at the prospect of meeting the red-haired girl. He put away the bucket and his way back across the farmyard through a horde of disgruntled chickens. When he opened the screen door, the smells were even richer and thicker inside, but it wasn't the delicious scents that made him catch his breath.

It was the girl. She was right there, hovering by the kitchen table, plates in one arm, halfway through setting it. When her eyes rested on him, they widened, and the scattered sunlight that filtered through the lace curtains at the window shattered inside them and turned them to the most brilliant green Zeb had ever seen. Her lips parted slightly, and every inch of color drained from her face, leaving the freckles sharply etched on her skin.

"Zeb, this is Marlene," said Sarah, beaming. "I told you about my niece."

Zeb nodded. "Pleased to meet you," he said.

She seemed to have gathered herself a little, her cheeks growing pinker. "P-pleased to meet you too," she stammered.

Her voice was hurried and husky, and there was something

jerky in her movements as she laid out the plates and took the seat furthest from him. Something that was almost like fear. It made her cheeks glow red, whatever it was, but somehow that didn't make her less attractive.

It made Zeb want to know more about the frightened secret hidden in her beautiful eyes.

Chapter Two

Anxiety sent a hot pang through Marlene's stomach as she stepped into the barn. The smell of hay and animals still lingered in its corners, but they were all outside now, the windows wide open to the cool November sunlight. Wooden benches filled the barn but for an aisle in the middle. And at the far end of the aisle, resplendent in his navy, Jeremy was waiting. His blue-gray eyes studying her with every step she took, a proud smile lighting up his face.

She was marrying the man she wanted, the man she loved. So why was her belly aching with fear? She tried to take a step forward and couldn't. A red-hot lance of pain stabbed through her again, and she couldn't move. The pain came again, a scream ripping through her, and she was waking up and sitting up in bed and her sheets were drenched in sweat.

Confused, Marlene stiffened, not wanting to wake Jeremy. But he wasn't here. She was in Sarah's house, and her belly was on fire.

"N-no." Marlene croaked the words out, staggering out of bed toward the little bathroom. She had only just reached the door when another terrible cramp seized her, doubling her over, panting. Sweat dripped from the end of her nose.

"No," she groaned again. She groped for the gas light, managed to turn it on, collapsed on the cool floor. When she pulled up her skirt, the difference in her belly was barely visible: just a tiny, tiny beginning of a bump, easily hidden under her baggy dress, the sole evidence of a little life within her.

A life that could be in peril now.

The next pain shot through her every nerve, striking her very toes with a force that wrenched a moan of agony through her. She leaned her head against the bathroom wall, waiting for it to pass, but it throbbed and boiled in her for what felt like a century before loosening its grip. By then, shuffling feet were sounding in her room, and the light there turned on.

"Marlene?"

"Help," Marlene croaked, panting in agony. "Help me. Help."

Sarah was suddenly beside her, struggling to bend down, her gnarled little hands gripping Marlene's. Her little black eyes were serious, steady. Marlene clung to the calmness in her like a lifeline. Somehow, she managed to utter the words.

"It's the *boppli*," she whispered. "Sarah, it's the *boppli*."

Sarah didn't ask questions. "Breathe," she said. "I'm going for the telephone. Zeb will have to come with his fast horse. We need to get you to the hospital."

"The hospital?" Marlene cried, aghast. "With *Englischers*?"

"Marlene." Sarah gripped her hands tightly, meeting her eyes. "Just because I have no grown *kinner* doesn't mean I was never pregnant. Trust me, *liebchen*. There is no time for anything else."

It seemed to take forever for the old lady to stagger out of the house to the little wooden shack in the back of the garden where the telephone was kept, yet once Sarah had reappeared in the bathroom – two horrific waves of pain later – and started helping Marlene into her clothes, it seemed to be only seconds before there was a hammering at the door.

"That'll be Zeb," said Sarah, tugging Marlene's *kapp* over her messy hair. "Can you walk?"

"*Jah*. I think so," Marlene groaned. "Oh, Sarah, my *boppli*..."

"It's all right. It's all in *Gott*'s hands," said Sarah. "Come, come. Hurry."

She pulled Marlene's arm over her shoulders and they staggered together down the stairs. When the door swung open, the lights on Zeb's buggy were filling the yard, and he was waiting on the porch. His eyes were deepest brown where they rested on Marlene, and there was no fear in them, just a calm as sturdy as his boots on the porch.

"I've got her," he told Sarah, reaching for Marlene's arm.

Marlene didn't want him to touch her. She didn't want him near her, not now, but another cramp gripped her, and she had no choice. Screaming, she doubled over, and Zeb put an arm around her. He smelled of hay and horses.

"It's all right," he said. "We'll get you safe. You'll be all right."

Marlene had no choice but to cling on to him, sobbing with agony. As reassuring as his voice was, as calmly as he spoke the words, she knew that they weren't true.

They weren't.

She had never known a buggy to move so quickly. Zeb never seemed to touch the whip to his horse, but the urgency in his voice must have been enough, because the landscape flew past them, the miles disappearing under the horse's hooves until they were wheeling into the parking area of the hospital and *Englischers* in blue scrubs came running out to meet them. Sarah was thanking Zeb, but Marlene could barely hear her. Her world had become a red haze of pain.

After that, there were gloved hands, and a gurney that wasn't quite soft enough, and lights. Voices all around her, pinpricks in her arms. They were shouting in English too fast for her to understand.

But she understood the eyes of the nurse who examined her and then looked up at her. They held a pain that struck straight into Marlene's heart and curled up there, sick and miserable and clinging.

They told her a few minutes later, in gentle English, with sympathetic touches. But by then she knew already.

She'd lost her baby.

When Sarah led Marlene out into the parking lot again, when the next day had brought light and birdsong back to Baker's Corner, it was Muddy who waited patiently between the shafts of the buggy. There was no need for a strong young horse today, Marlene realized miserably. It was already much too late.

Zeb was standing at Muddy's head, stroking the old horse's ears absently as Marlene and Sarah approached.

"*Gut* morning," he said, sounding cheerful. He gave her a broad smile. "I'm so glad that you can come back home today."

Marlene tried her best to smile back, but she couldn't. Tears choked her. It took all of her strength to keep them out of her eyes; Zeb had no idea why she was grieving. It wouldn't be proper to tell him about her lost child. He must think she had some simple digestive issue, when the truth was much more heart-wrenching.

"Marlene's still feeling a little poorly," said Sarah. "But she'll be all right."

"Of course," said Zeb. He reached out a hand to Marlene. "Let me help you into the buggy."

She didn't want to touch him, just as she hadn't wanted the support of his arms last night, but she knew she didn't have the strength to climb into the buggy herself. She tentatively laid her hand in his own. It was big, warm, calloused by work, yet when the great thick fingers folded over hers, they had a tenderness she hadn't been expecting. She leaned on it as she heaved her battered body into the seat of the buggy, letting go of Zeb's hand as quickly as she could.

"Smooth driving, please, Zeb," said Sarah. "Marlene's still in quite a bit of pain."

"*Ach*, I'm sorry to hear it," said Zeb. He hopped up into the driver's seat and gathered the reins in his giant hands. "Hear that, Muddy old boy? You need to be your quiet old self, now."

The horse jogged slowly back along country lanes, carrying Marlene back toward the house. She leaned her head back, eyes closed, feeling more exhausted than she'd ever been in all her life. Her body felt ripped – as if some clawed hand had torn that baby out of her – but it was nothing compared to her heart. They hadn't even been able to give her the baby to hold, to say goodbye to. It was still much too early. The nurse had been gentle as she'd slipped a needle into Marlene's arm so gently that she barely felt it.

"You could try again," she'd said, kindly. "In a few weeks, you'll be as good as new."

Marlene didn't know what that meant anymore. And she knew that she would not be trying again, not willingly, in any case. For the feeling that boiled in her heart – a feeling ten, a hundred, a million times worse than the grief of losing her child – was the sick realization that part of her was relieved not to have brought that baby alive and screaming into the world. She didn't want her infant to share her fate.

She didn't want to give Jeremy a child.

A single tear ran down her cheek. Sarah gripped her hand tightly, rubbing her fingers to reassure her, and she wiped her tear away with a quick, shaky movement.

She kept no track of the time; it didn't matter now. Nothing mattered except the anguish that wrapped a heavy shroud around her heart. It could have been seconds or days later that they arrived back in the farmyard. Sarah bustled down off the buggy, talking about cakes and coffee and making Marlene's favorite dish for dinner as she disappeared into the house.

Zeb moved more slowly. Climbing down from the driver's seat, he opened the door for Marlene and held out a hand.

"Are you all right?" he said, softly.

Marlene found her eyes raising themselves to his. As sturdy and simple as his face was, his eyes were mesmerizing. Their hypnotic mixture of green and brown drew her in, made her cling a little tighter to the hand he'd offered.

For an instant, she wanted to tell him everything – and not just about the baby. She wanted to tell him about Jeremy, and her flight to Baker's Corner, and her fears that Jeremy would come looking for her.

She couldn't, of course. She'd never told anyone. She never could.

"*Jah*," she managed, finding that smile she always managed to plaster on, no matter how appalling her heart felt. "Just a little sore and tired."

"*Gut.*" Zeb squeezed her hand, smiling; she felt the warmth of it strike right down to the very bottom of her soul.

He helped her down, and she shook her head minutely as he

led her in small, shuffling steps across the front porch. It had to be the medication they'd given her that was making her feel this strange, because it wasn't comfort or interest.

It couldn't be.

Chapter Three

"There." Sarah's quick, gentle, patting hands tucked the sheets neatly around Marlene's aching body. She reached up to plump up the pillows, her apron gently brushing Marlene's arms where they lay folded protectively over her belly. "Are you comfortable? Is that too warm?"

Marlene tried to smile. "*Nee, danke*. That's perfect."

"*Wunderlich.*" Sarah paused, her eyes sweeping the bedroom from corner to corner, making sure that everything was arranged just as Marlene needed it: a novel on the nightstand, a cup of warm milk beside it, the quilt within easy reach. "Do you need anything else?"

"*Nee, danke*. You've been so *gut* to me, Sarah," said Marlene. "*Danke*."

"*Ach,* of course, *liebchen.*" Sarah gripped Marlene's hand and gave it a fond little squeeze. She paused for a minute. "Shall I write to Jeremy about the *boppli* for you?"

"*Nee,*" Marlene cried, a lance of fear running through her body.

Sarah blinked, surprised. "Sorry," she said. "I just thought…"

"*Nee, nee.* Don't apologize." Marlene took a shaky breath, trying to calm herself. "*Danke* for offering, but don't worry. I'd rather write to him myself."

Those shrewd little black eyes were studying her again, and Marlene wondered how much Sarah suspected. "All right," she said at length. "I'll just be in the sewing room if you need me."

"*Danke,*" said Marlene.

Sarah shut the door quietly behind her, and Marlene leaned back on her pillows, closing her eyes as a wave of exhaustion washed over her. Maybe she should just tell her aunt everything. The thought made shame rise up in her, flooding her heart with something bitter and sharp. How could she? Sarah would know then that she was a fool, a worthless, stupid little fool, and that everything was her own fault. Tears stung her eyes. She *was* a fool, and now she felt she was a killer, too. She was the one who'd married Jeremy—and that choice had led to the death of her baby.

The summer breeze blowing in through the open window was fragrant, pleasant; her pillows were soft, and the medication had made the pain subside a little. Marlene tried to empty her mind, breathing deeply as she fought for sleep, but nothing could stop the memory from crawling out of the darkness. It sank its bitter claws into her and dragged her into its ugly depths. And she couldn't stop herself from being transported back to the night that she'd realized she had no choice but to run.

It began like it always did; when Jeremy got in from a day's work in the fields. Marlene had done her best to do everything just right. She always did, but that night was extra special. That night, she couldn't do anything to make him angry. She'd run a nervous hand over her belly, which still felt utterly flat then, as she waited for the beef pie to finish baking. She had big news. None of her mistakes could ruin this evening.

She made sure that everything was perfect: the table set, the kitchen spotless, all of his favorite dishes warm and freshly served by the time his boots sounded on the front porch. Taking her place beside his spot at the head of the table, Marlene was trembling a little when the front door opened. Jeremy stepped inside. He was a tall, angular man who seemed to be built out of stone: his shoulders rippling like boulders under his shirt, skin white as marble, a face as hard and stern as a windblown crag, his eyes two caves that glowed with blue-gray luminescence. They swept across the kitchen, and Marlene held her breath. If he found something now...

He didn't. Marlene allowed herself a sip of air as he strode across the room and collapsed in his chair. She dutifully grasped the gravy boat and poured just the right amount over his slice of beef pie. Jeremy said nothing as she stepped back, so she took her cue and settled down into her chair beside him.

He didn't like to be interrupted while he ate. Too nervous to eat, Marlene picked at her own pie, despite the perfect creaminess of the filling and the golden, buttery crust. Jeremy paused only to take repeated sips from the flask he always carried in his pocket. The stale smell of alcohol began to grow in the kitchen, and Marlene felt a sting of fear in the frigid silence. Was tonight really the best night for her to do this?

She had only finished a few bites of her pie when he pushed his plate aside and raked her with a swift glance. "What's wrong with you, woman?" he barked. "Why aren't you eating the *gut* food I've provided for you? I work hard with my own bare hands to give that to you."

His voice snapped over her shoulders like a whip. She raised her chin, her heart hammering. This might be the only chance she'd get.

"Jeremy," she said, as meekly as she could. "I'm pregnant."

He froze halfway through another swig from the flask.

Lowering it slowly, he turned his eyes on her, and she flinched as though she'd been struck.

"You're *what?*"

His voice was low and husky. Marlene took a deep breath, trying to calm her fluttering heart. "We're having a *boppli*," she said, smiling. "I'm having a *boppli*, Jeremy. We're going to be a family."

Jeremy pushed back his chair and rose, towering over her, swaying slightly. "Whose is it?" he snarled.

Marlene felt her face grow ice cold. "It's yours, of course," she said. "Jeremy – you know me. You know I would never..."

"Is it Joshua's?" Jeremy snarled.

Marlene shook her head, utterly bewildered. Why would he even think she would have an affair with the farm hand? "*Nee, nee!*" she cried. "Jeremy..."

It was too late to placate him. It was no use reasoning with him; it never had been. He seized his plate and hurled it across the kitchen, and when it shattered on the opposite wall, all of Marlene's dreams of this baby somehow fixing everything that was broken between them seemed to shatter with it. She scrambled to her feet, but there was no escaping him. The first blow rang heavily across her left ear, throwing her to the ground, stars popping in front of her eyes. Then he was upon her, and his fists were slamming into her. Into her back. Her ribs. Her side. Her belly.

In his rage, he was always careful to mark her where it wouldn't be seen.

Three mornings later, before dawn could break, she had slipped out from under the drunken sound of his snoring. She stole a few dollars from the pocket of the pants he'd thrown down on the ground, grabbed a change of clothes, and walked to the bus stop to save her baby.

And it had all been too late.

Marlene was safe in Sarah's spare bedroom, but she could still feel those punches slamming into her flesh, hear the sickly sound of his knuckles meeting her skin. She rolled over, covering her head with her arms, and sobbed and sobbed.

Ach, Gott. Ach, Gott! How can You ever forgive me?

The scream of her soul seemed to echo in empty darkness.

Chapter Four

The sunlight on Marlene's back was warm and soothing where it poured in through the high barn window. She took deep breaths, leaning her head deeply into the warm, fragrant flank of her aunt's dairy cow. The smells of hay and warm milk and animals surrounded her. They reminded her of a happier time; perhaps the only happy times of her lonely little childhood, when her ailing father had died at last after a long illness during which a heartless nurse had cared for her, and she'd been sent to live with Sarah and her late husband. Her uncle used to sweep her up into the hay rack and let her sit there laughing while he fed the animals and milked the cow.

Now it was her hands that coaxed the long white streaks of milk from the cow's soft udder, filling the bucket with foaming fluid. The cow chewed her cud happily as Marlene worked, and somewhere among the peace of the barn, she began to feel something like the bovine's obvious contentment. The weeks that had passed since her miscarriage had healed her body almost completely, yet she felt that the gaping wound in her heart would bleed forever.

She let out a deep sigh, pausing to shake out her fingers. Jeremy hadn't let her keep a dairy cow back home. Fear ran through her. Jeremy still hadn't found her, yet she couldn't shake the feeling that it was only a matter of time.

The barn door creaked, and Marlene jumped, making the milk bucket rattle. She grabbed it, keeping it from tipping over.

"Whoa there!" Zeb's gentle voice sounded with laughter. "Sorry, Marlene. I didn't mean to startle you."

Marlene took a deep breath. She turned around, and he was standing just a few feet behind her, his face transfixed by one of those big, easy grins that seemed to come so naturally to him. Looking up at him from her milking stool, Marlene was reminded once again of just how massive Zeb really was. He was easily the tallest man she'd ever seen and built like a carthorse; there was nothing graceful in his lumbering movement as he came over to her, but when he held out a hand to help her up, the gesture was tender.

Marlene still didn't want to take his hand. She pushed back her milking stool, gripped the bucket and rose to her feet. The movement tugged at something in her abdomen, and she couldn't hold back a tiny gasp of pain. Zeb gripped her elbow, supporting her gently as she wobbled for a second, taking the handle of the milk bucket out of her hands.

"All right?" he asked, easily. There was concern in his voice, but also calm.

Marlene looked up at him. Her heart hammered as she realized how close he was; how steady. "I'm fine," she said.

"*Gut.*" Zeb stepped back, letting her go. His hand lingered near hers for a moment, and for a wild second, she thought she might take it. She wondered what it would feel like to have his big, warm fingers intertwine with hers. Her heart raced, and she swallowed her feelings back.

You're still married, Marlene, she reminded herself. Giving him a quick, polite smile, she stepped aside, opening a gap of a few feet between them. "Did Sarah send you to fetch me?" she asked.

He blinked, and the intent left his eyes. His smile grew breezy. "*Jah*, she says that breakfast is ready when you've done the milking," he said.

"Well, let's go, then," said Marlene.

She fell into step beside him, and it took her a few seconds to realize that she was smiling. Not the smile that she so consciously forced onto her face all the time, but something real and genuine that had come from deep inside her and warmed her from the soles of her feet to her very lips.

She looked over at Zeb where he walked beside her with graceless strides, surrounded by an aura of peace. And she had to tell herself, again, that she was still married.

No matter how she tossed and turned that night, sleep refused to come to Marlene. She had tried to tire herself out by reading late, but even now with the little gas lamp on the nightstand turned off and the bedroom cloaked in soothing darkness, she found herself staring at the silver lines that the moonlight traced around the edges of the curtains. Her eyes, however, weren't staring at Sarah's spare bedroom.

They were seeing the steady figure of Zeb walking across the fields that afternoon, a young calf slung over his shoulders, his big hands wrapped around its feet as its mother trotted along behind him. The mother didn't seem overly worried that Zeb was carrying her calf; it was as if even the animals knew that they could trust him.

Even Marlene could sense that there was something about him that was as different to Jeremy as a cornerstone is to a firestorm. She wanted to trust him, and the way that he looked at her... It lacked the blazing intensity, the hungriness of Jeremy's gaze, but she knew that he would court her if she let him.

Her heart began to pound. How could she even be thinking of these things? She couldn't keep lying to Sarah forever. She'd fled here in desperation for her unborn child, but she knew she couldn't stay. And even if she did, Jeremy would find her. It had been weeks now. Her time was running out. She had to...

There was a sound from outside that cut her thoughts off short. Marlene froze, aware that she was trembling. Had she imagined it?

No. There it was again; a rustle, followed by the unmistakable snap of a breaking twig. In the country night, it sounded like a gunshot.

Marlene's mouth was bone dry. Jeremy had found her. *No!* She tried to take a deep breath, but it was as if lava had been poured into her lungs. *No, Marlene! Stay calm.* Swallowing, she wondered if she should wake Sarah. Perhaps they could call the police −

Something rattled outside. The gate. He was coming through the gate, and if he came in here, he would kill her, but more than that, *Sarah*. Sarah would try to protect her, Marlene knew, and Jeremy would break the old woman like a twig.

She couldn't lie in bed anymore. She had to go out and confront him, tell her to take her home and not hurt anyone else, without waking Sarah.

Slipping out of bed, Marlene grabbed a flashlight from the drawer of her nightstand. She tucked her feet into her sheepskin slippers and padded down the stairs, keeping the flashlight half covered with her hand, allowing only a crack of light so she could make her way into the kitchen without falling. Pausing there, she strained her ears to listen, surrounded by darkness except for the square of muffled light cast through the curtained window by the gas lamp on the porch. Something was moving around in the garden; she could hear it rustling. A shadow flitted over the window, and Marlene jumped, her veins afire. She juggled the flashlight for a precarious moment, only just keeping her grip on it.

She had to act now before he came through the front door. Stepping forward carefully, her heart pounding in her ears, she reached for the front door. It let out a drawn-out moan when she pushed it open. Hairs rose on the back of her neck, and in the yellow light of the gas lamp, she swept her eyes across the garden. His figure seemed to be everywhere – crouching in the shadow of the nearest bush, looming behind the lemon tree, rushing back behind the washing line.

"J-Jeremy?" Marlene whispered. She'd meant to call softly, but she could hardly manage more than a wheeze.

There was no response, but she could still hear something scratching around by the garbage can around the back of the house. Mustering her courage, she stepped forward. A cool breeze that spoke of fall wrapped itself around her ankles, tracing frozen fingers up her calves as she shone the torch into the garden ahead of her. It stirred the branches, making them look like arms that would reach out and grab her. What would he do when he saw her? Would he close his hard fingers around her face so that she could barely breathe? Would he seize the soft skin on the inside of her arm and twist until it turned blue?

Would he just strangle her this time?

She'd nearly reached the garbage can. She could still hear the shuffling, the low scratching of something against the metal surface. He must be hiding back there, ready to pounce on her.

"Jeremy," she cried, her voice an anguished yelp, and shone the light into the darkness behind it. A pair of eyes looked back at her, glowing gray and blue in the flashlight's beam, and teeth flashed. Marlene staggered back. The raccoon fled, its fat tail following it into the safety of the bushes.

Marlene's heart was thumping so fast that she could feel it reverberate through her body. She laid a hand on it, trying to calm it, tears of horror cooling on her cheeks. It was just a raccoon this time, but what about next time?

The image of Jeremy storming into that peaceful little house and seizing her dear Sarah was unthinkable. Marlene swallowed hard.

Was she doing the right thing by being here at all?

Chapter Five

The next morning came with hardly any sleep at all. Where Marlene stood kneading a lump of bread dough, she felt as tired and wrung-out and faded as the dishcloth over her shoulder; except the dishcloth, she was quite sure, probably didn't feel stressed as well. She flipped the dough over on the counter, pressing her knuckles deep into the soft, giving surface. There was a little solace in the familiar movement. Only a little.

Stiff footsteps on the stairs announced the arrival of a sleepy-eyed Sarah, who blinked at her in the shallow dawn light.

"Marlene?" She reached for the light, turning on the gas ceiling lights. "What are you doing up so early?"

Marlene turned, groping for the most brilliant of her false smiles. "*Gut* morning, Sarah," she trilled. "I woke up early, so I decided I'd get started on the bread. We're already getting low."

She dumped the dough into a bowl and covered it with the dishcloth. Frayed at the edges, just like her. Turning to Sarah, she tried to maintain the smile. "Can I make you some coffee?"

Sarah studied her with glittering eyes for a moment, then sank into a chair. "*Danke*," she said. "That would be nice."

Marlene filled the kettle and lifted it onto the gas stove, starting the little blue flame beneath it. The weight of what she had to do was burning inside her; she couldn't hold back any longer. If she didn't speak now, she might never have the courage.

"So," she said, as nonchalantly as she could manage, "I have some *gut* news for you, Sarah."

Her aunt gave her a wary smile. "What's that?"

"Well, I think I'm well enough to travel now and it's time for me to go back home."

The thought was utterly wrenching. She couldn't believe she'd actually spoken the words; she hardly knew if it really was home that she'd go back to, but either way, she couldn't stay here and put Sarah in danger.

Sarah stared at her, unflinchingly. "*Nee*," she said calmly. "You're not going back home."

"Sarah." Marlene laughed. "What on earth do you mean? Of course, I'm going back home. I'm all better again, and Jeremy will be missing me." That much was true; in a horrid, clinging way. "We could try for another *boppli*," she managed, only faltering a little on the last word.

Sarah folded her arms, resting them on the table. "You're not going anywhere until you tell me what's happening," she said.

"What do you mean?" asked Marlene, but her facade was crumbling; she could feel it slipping away from her, like a diseased bandage being ripped off an infected wound.

Sarah leaned back in her chair. "I saw you creeping around the *haus* last night."

"Oh, that." Marlene laughed. "*Jah*, that was silly of me. I heard noises outside, and they gave me a fright. It was just a silly old raccoon, that's all."

Sarah shook her head. Her voice held a reprimand, but no anger. "Marlene, please don't lie to me," she said. "I know something's been going on between you and Jeremy. I need you to tell me the real reason why you came to Baker's Corner."

Marlene stared at her. Every lie she could think of, every story she had so often concocted over the years that she'd been married to Jeremy, all shriveled up and vanished in her heart when she looked into Sarah's sharp, dark eyes.

"Marlene." Sarah's tone was gentle. "Sit down, please, and tell me everything."

Marlene felt wobbly. She slid into a chair opposite Sarah, staring at her aunt, as the old woman went on. "Something's been different about you ever since you came back to Baker's Corner," Sarah said. "You haven't been yourself – especially not last night. I expect the truth."

Marlene knew she did. She could feel the truth inside her, pounding against the gates of her terror in great crashing waves, filling her eyes, running down her cheeks in hot salt tears. Sarah leaned over, gripping her hands. "Please, *liebchen*," she begged. "Please. Just tell me."

Marlene couldn't hold those waves back any longer. She bowed her head, shame filling her like nausea.

"Jeremy hurts me, Sarah," she whispered.

Sarah fell completely silent, but her hands trembled on Marlene's. When Marlene looked up, her aunt's eyes were filled with tears. The compassion in them gave her the strength to keep talking, the truth pouring out of her at last after years of being trapped inside.

"It started even before we were married," she said. "He would grab me if I tried to walk away from him, or if we argued or if there was just something annoying him about me. At first, I thought he was just passionate. I was so happy to be wanted like that. But after we were married, it turned into something else, or maybe it had been something else all along."

She couldn't have stopped now if she tried; it poured out of her at last, like pus from an abscess. "Our wedding night was the first time he held me down. And we'd been married a week when I burned his dinner for the first time, the same day that the plow hitch broke in the fields, and he struck me. Since then..." She shook her head. "It never stopped. Not even the night that I told him I was pregnant."

Sarah's voice was steady despite the tears that weighed it down. "That was when you decided to leave."

"I had to. I was so foolish, Sarah." Tears choked her. "I'm such a fool. If only I'd left before telling him, then maybe my *boppli...*"

"*Nee.*" Sarah's grip on her hands grew steady. "Marlene, *nee.* You can't think like that."

"You know that it's true," said Marlene. "It's all my fault. And now... and now I have to get away from here, because if Jeremy finds me, he'll hurt you, too, just like he hurt my *boppli.*"

"You're not going anywhere," said Sarah.

"Sarah..."

"*Nee.* It's final, Marlene," said Sarah firmly. "Jeremy isn't going to find you here."

40

"What if he does?" Marlene cried. "I can't have anything happen to you."

"Nothing is going to happen to me. *Gott* will protect us," said Sarah. She squeezed Marlene's hands, smiling at her, her eyes drying. "*Liebchen*, even if Jeremy finds you, then we'll deal with him. Together."

Marlene closed her eyes, feeling her heart fill with something that was much bigger and warmer than fear. She smiled at Marlene, the tears cascading down her cheeks.

"Together," she whispered.

Chapter Six

Marlene's pen hovered over the sheet of paper on the kitchen table in front of her. "Maybe this isn't such a *gut* idea," she said.

Sarah was kneading some bread dough opposite her, the small, gnarled fingers working the lumpy mixture into something smooth and beautiful. She glanced up, her hands working automatically. "We've been over this a thousand times in the past two days, Marlene," she said gently. "There's no reason to keep delaying this any further. Thoughts of Jeremy have been haunting you ever since you first came here, and it's not healthy. You need to find out what he's doing so that you can have some peace of mind. Why – I believe he's so ashamed of what he's done, he'll never try to bother you again in your life."

"Still," said Marlene reluctantly. "I don't want to put my best friend in danger."

"Mona must be missing you," said Sarah.

Marlene sighed. "I miss her, too," she said. "She's such a *wunderlich* friend. I didn't tell her why I was leaving Jeremy, just that I had to go and that she couldn't tell anyone where I'd gone. She didn't even want an explanation. She just told me that whatever I needed, she would help me."

"Now then," said Sarah. "She'll be able to tell you what he's up to. Then you'll know for sure that he's not looking for you."

"And if he is?"

"Then we'll deal with it. Together," said Sarah, smiling bravely. "Just like I said."

Marlene nodded slowly, turning back to the page in front of her. Sarah was right. She couldn't bear not knowing whether Jeremy was coming after her, and the only person she trusted back in her old home was sweet, kind Mona.

"I'll use a different name," said Marlene. "One that Mona will guess at, but no one else will. That way the postman won't get curious – he's probably friends with Jeremy. Everyone is friends with Jeremy."

"*Gut* idea," said Sarah.

Marlene lowered her pen to the page and began to write.

.   .   .

My dear friend,

I pray with all my heart that you are well and happy. I miss you so much, and I wish I could see you again, but I don't know how it would be possible. Either way, may Gott *be with you every day of your life.*

I'm mostly all right here with Sarah, but I lost my boppli. *I know that this was my husband's fault, and I'm afraid that he's going to come looking for me – and do something terrible to poor Sarah. Please, Mona, I know this is a risky thing to ask of you, but you're the bravest person I know and the only one that I can turn to. If you would, please write me back and tell me what Jeremy is doing. Is he searching for me? I have to know, because if he is, I must get out of here. I must make sure that Sarah is safe.*

Forgive me if this causes you any trouble. I pray for you always.

All my love,

Emma Fisher

She showed the letter to Sarah, who nodded. "It looks *gut*, except that you're not going anywhere if Jeremy comes looking," she said firmly.

"Sarah..."

The old woman talked over her. "Who's Emma Fisher?"

Marlene laughed. "*Ach*, Mona will know. She has five *kinner,* and she told me once – on a hard day when all of them were fighting and making a mess – that she was going to move to another town and start a new life as the childless Emma Fisher. It's become a joke between us."

"Excellent," said Sarah. "I'll give it to the postman in the morning. Make sure you put that name as the sender on the envelope, too. That way, Jeremy won't be able to find you."

Marlene felt a pang of terror grip her. She was almost certain that nothing was going to stop him from tracking her down.

Marlene added another pancake to the growing golden stack on the kitchen counter by the stove. The sweet, buttery smell filled the kitchen as she scooped another expert spoonful from the bowl and drizzled it into the pan, watching contentedly as the mixture began to bubble and puff up just the way she liked it. Jeremy hated pancakes. It had been a long time since she'd made them; even at Sarah's house, the thought of making them made her feel dizzy with fear. Yet today was a perfect pancake day – a cool day that spoke of coming winter, with a mist that alternated with drizzling – and she wasn't about to let it pass her by.

The front door creaked open, and heavy footsteps announced Zeb's arrival. Marlene found herself smiling by accident when she looked up at him.

"*Gut* morning," she said, with more enthusiasm than she meant.

Zeb's eyes widened as he studied the stack of pancakes on the counter. "It must be," he said, "if those *wunderlich* pancakes are involved."

Marlene laughed. "Wash your hands and sit down," she said. "I'm nearly done with these. Sarah will be up from the dairy in a minute with the cream."

"*Ach, nee,*" Zeb's eyes filled with worry. "It's so cold outside. I should have brought the cream in myself."

"Don't worry, Zeb," said Marlene. "She said that a little walk would keep her old joints oiled."

"I suppose," said Zeb, reluctantly sinking into a chair.

Marlene couldn't help gazing at the care and concern in his two-toned eyes. She found her heart wandering, thinking of what it would be like to get up every morning and make pancakes for this man, this strange, hulking giant of a man with his gentle eyes and soft voice. Zeb seemed to notice she was staring. He looked up, and when their eyes met, a smile crept over his face that warmed her from her toes to the top of her head.

A blush crept to her cheeks. *You're still married, Marlene*, she reminded herself, forcibly flipping the pancake.

The door opened again, letting in a burst of cold air, and

Sarah came in with a jug of cream in her hands and something tucked under her arm. Zeb immediately jumped up and took the jug from her, holding the door at the same time. "I could have done that for you, Sarah," he said reproachfully.

"*Ach*, Zeb," Sarah laughed, a small hand patting the vastness of his chest as she limped inside. "I've hired you as a farm hand, you know, not a nanny. You are sweet, though." She sniffed. "Pancakes. You haven't made those for us since you were a little *maidel*, Marlene."

"Well, I thought it was about time," laughed Marlene, trying her best to keep her eyes off Zeb. "Sit down, you two. They're all ready."

"*Gut*. I'm starving," said Sarah. She lowered herself stiffly into a chair and watched in appreciation as Marlene piled pancakes onto her plate. "Oh, *jah* – I have a letter for you, Marlene."

Her hand slipped as she was busy setting Zeb's plate down in front of him. It rattled, spilling pancakes all over the table. Fear clutched at her, and for a split second, she expected Zeb to raise a hand to her. Instead, he looked up, his eyes filled with worry.

"Are you all right?" he asked.

"*Jah, jah*," said Marlene, laughing breezily, a well-practiced laugh. "Sorry – my hand slipped."

"My timing wasn't very *gut*, either," said Sarah. Her tone was light, but when she met Sarah's eyes, her gaze was filled with apology. She took the envelope out from under her arm and laid it on the kitchen table. "There you are."

"*Danke*," said Marlene. Zeb was still watching her, but she somehow couldn't bring herself to sit down. "Ah – I'll be back down for breakfast in a minute."

She grabbed the envelope and hurried upstairs.

Chapter Seven

"Marlene?" Zeb's voice pursued her, but she ran into her bedroom, slammed the door, and fell trembling into the armchair by her bed. It took her two attempts with her shaking hands to tear the envelope open.

Dear Emma,

I was so, so relieved to hear from you. I'm so happy to hear you're safe with Sarah! Gott will protect you and keep His hand of love over you, my friend.

Marlene gave her head a faint shake. She knew that she didn't deserve God's protection.

. . .

I have been keeping an eye on your husband ever since you left. To be honest with you, things are not going well with him. He's drinking openly now and most of the community knows it. He's lost a lot of friends; in fact, I don't think I've seen him sober ever since you left. He's acting stranger and stranger, too.

Sometimes he disappears for days at a time and no one knows where he's gone. Emma, I don't care what anyone here says about you. I know that you did nothing wrong, and I'm afraid that he might be looking for you. But please don't leave. Stay where you are. You're safest there. Besides, the bishop and the deacons have noticed now that something is wrong with your husband, and they're investigating him. I'm sure that they're going to put him under discipline, and they're keeping a watchful eye on him. They won't let him go and find you.

Trust me, please. Stay right where you are.

I pray for you all the time, and I know that Gott *is with you.*

Love,

Mona.

Marlene allowed herself a long breath out. It was some small relief that the bishop had an eye on Jeremy; he was a long, gaunt, stern-eyed man who might just be able to keep him under control. Yet she'd hardly allowed herself to feel that relief before her heart was flooded with an aching wave of guilt. Her eye darted back up the page. *Things are not going well with him... lost a lot of friends... something is wrong... don't think I've seen him sober since you left.*

It was her fault. Jeremy was falling apart, the man she'd married and pledged to love and care for her entire life was crumbling, and she was the one responsible. She was the culprit. She had done this to him. Tears burned her eyes, and she folded to the floor, her shoulders trembling. She'd killed her baby. She was destroying her husband's life.

If she'd been a better person, she could have made her marriage work. She wouldn't have run off the way she had. She would have stayed and somehow, someway, made it through.

So much of her believed she was worthless. But there was something about the way Zeb looked at her, something about the compassion in Sarah's eyes, that made her want to believe differently. But at point, she had no idea how to change her beliefs. Her warped image of herself was too deeply ingrained —but oh, how she wished it were different.

The group of steers milled around in the pen, shaking their curly heads in consternation as they watched Zeb and Marlene walk inside. Zeb held the gate for her; Marlene's arms were full, between the gigantic plastic drenching syringe she had under her arm, the clipboard with its list of animals in one hand, and the heavy bottle of medicine in the other. The steers gave them suspicious looks out of their big dark eyes and trotted to the opposite end of the pen.

"I've been telling Sarah for years that she needs a chute," said Marlene, bending down to put the things on the ground. "That would make this so much easier."

"*Ach*, it'll be all right," said Zeb patiently. "There are only seven of them, and they're barely yearlings. I'll grab them and you can dose them."

"Grab them?" Marlene looked doubtfully at the row of shaggy brown bodies. "Aren't they a little big for that?"

Zeb folded his arms. Marlene was reminded, again, of how truly big he was. "I think we'll give it a try," he said mildly.

"All right," said Marlene.

She helped him to shepherd one of the steers into a corner. As soon as the big animal was separated from the others, Marlene cried, "All right! Get him!"

Zeb shook his head slowly. "*Nee, nee*," he said, not unkindly. "Give him a minute and he won't jump at all."

Slowly, he reached out a hand the size of a shovel toward the steer. He started to gently scratch his ears with his fingertips. At first, the steer flinched, its eyes widening in fear, but the more Zeb scratched, the more the steer seemed to relax. Marlene couldn't take her eyes off the animal. The lines of its body softened, its head lowering, lips twitching in delight at Zeb's touch.

"*Gut* boy," said Zeb mildly. "Now, you don't need to be scared. This medicine is going to do you *gut*." He took a step forward and slipped his arms around the steer's neck. The steer twitched slightly, its head cradled in Zeb's powerful arms, and stood still.

"All right," said Zeb. "Dose him."

"Don't you want to grab his ear? Or his nose?" said Marlene.

"*Nee*, it won't be necessary," said Zeb.

Marlene wasn't so sure that the steer was going to keep its head still; she thought it might jerk back when it saw the syringe and ram its hard poll into Zeb's nose. But he smiled at her. "It's all right, Marlene," he said.

She filled the syringe and approached slowly. The steer regarded her with a nervous eye, but Zeb was scratching the underside of its jaw now, and after a moment, it relaxed. Marlene could hardly believe it. She slid the tip of the dosing syringe into the corner of the steer's mouth and squirted the medicine onto the back of its tongue. The steer gave a little sneeze of disgust, but didn't pull away, still enjoying the scratching.

"I can't believe it!" Marlene laughed. "He's like a pet for you."

Zeb let the steer go, and it trotted off to join its friends. "*Ach*, he knows I won't hurt him," he said. "Let's get the next one."

Marlene fell into step beside him, unable to stop herself from gazing up at his calm face, his serene eyes. She couldn't let herself do this. She couldn't even tell Zeb that she was still married, that she was running from her own husband, and yet every moment she spent with him was a moment that she wanted to live again.

She knew exactly how that steer felt.

"That's it," said Marlene, ticking off a number on the clipboard she held in front of her as her eyes swept the group of steers. "That's the last one."

Zeb smiled, trying to focus on her words instead of the musical sound of her voice. It wasn't singsong, exactly; nor did it have a high pitch. It just sounded as though, at any moment, she might burst into song. He could have listened to it all day.

"*Danke*," he said. "I appreciate your help. Your aunt always tries but I'm so worried she'll get knocked over."

"*Jah*, I can't think how she'd be able to do it." Marlene laughed, and the sound fell on Zeb's soul like the first raindrops after a drought. "But I'm sure she believes she can."

"She's never been one for sitting still, your aunt," said Zeb.

"*Nee*. I suppose it's part of what makes her special."

Marlene smiled up at him, and Zeb's breath caught in his chest. He could gaze into her eyes forever. He fought every urge in him that wanted to take her hand as they walked back to the house side by side. The fact that she left inches, instead of feet, of space open between them already felt like a little victory; she seemed so much more comfortable around him now. Zeb didn't know what had happened that made her so nervous, but he was glad to see the fear in her fading.

Still, as he laughed and joked with her, he could see in her eyes that there was something she wasn't telling him. More than anything in the world, he longed to know what was going on in Marlene's heart, but he knew it wouldn't come quickly.

He was ready to wait. Whenever she chose to trust him, he'd be ready.

Chapter Eight

Snap.

Marlene's eyes opened instantly, yanking her from a dream filled with green-brown eyes and a gentle smile. She lay still, breathing slowly, wrapped in her quilt against the chill of fall. That dream had left her feeling like she'd just drunk a mug of warm milk and honey; safe and sleepy. She nestled a little deeper into her pillows, hearing more snapping and rustling from outside. It was just the raccoon again, she was sure.

She was going to go back to sleep, and then she was going to wake up the next morning and make scrambled eggs for Zeb and Sarah, and everything was going to be just fine. If only she could get back into that dream. She turned her face into the pillow, groping for the dregs of that beautiful dream even though there was a part of her that knew she shouldn't be dreaming about going for long walks in the fields with Zebadiah Hartzler.

It nearly worked. She was just starting to feel the warm arms of sleep around her consciousness when the window broke.

The sound of it shattered the sleepy darkness of the house, a thundering noise that Marlene felt in every fiber of her body. She was on her feet and grabbing for her flashlight almost before she could think. Frozen, she listened to the tinkle of falling glass. Something thudded in the kitchen, and her heart turned over. *Sarah*.

"Marlene?" Sarah cried.

"I'm coming!" Marlene shouted, switching on the flashlight. Its light swooped crazily as she ran out into the hallway, painting the familiar objects – the cuckoo clock on the wall, the floral wallpaper, the smooth floorboards – in a strange and frightening light. Her bare feet thundered on the floor as she ran to Sarah's room. The light was lit, and her aunt was silhouetted in the doorway, her dark eyes wide.

"What's happening?" she cried.

"I don't know. Hush, please," Marlene begged. "Please, hush. I don't know where he is."

Sarah blanched. "Jeremy?" she whispered.

"I don't know. Please stay in your room," said Marlene. "I'll go and see."

"Marlene!" Sarah hissed.

Marlene was already tiptoeing downstairs, playing the flashlight left and right ahead of her, expecting at any minute for a pair of gray-blue eyes to stare out at her and a set of strong fingers to seize her by the neck. But all was silent around her now, and nothing moved as she slipped into the kitchen. Her heart was still pounding. She took deep breaths. Maybe it was the raccoon after all, she considered, or a tree branch or a bird. There had never been anything to be afraid of in this house before.

Marlene summoned her courage. Keeping her back tucked to the wall between the doorway and one of the cabinets, she lifted her flashlight and shone it across the kitchen just once. Once was enough to show her everything she needed to see, lit up brutally by the cold, swinging light. The shattered, jagged edges of the broken window, jutting up like glass teeth in the night. The trail of shattered porcelain where the salt and pepper pots had once stood, broken into a thousand tiny shards across the table now. The long gouge in Sarah's prized mahogany table, an heirloom from her grandmother. And lying by Marlene's feet, simple and sinister as a death threat, the brick.

It had been hurled by human hands, that much was for certain, and Marlene didn't have to guess who could have done it. She fled back up the stairs, bent double below the windows, expecting at any moment another great crash and the flung missile to strike her down. Flashlight off, she tripped on the stairs and fell; the sound of it seemed to her ears like a bomb, calling him to her location. Any moment now he was going to appear, and his hard hands would clasp around her ankle and jerk her back. But somehow, he didn't appear. Somehow, she kept on going until she was stumbling into Sarah's room, pushing her aunt inside, slamming the door and shoving the armchair up against it.

"What is it, child?" Sarah cried.

"It's Jeremy," Marlene panted. "He's put a brick through the window."

It was a long, cold, terrifying night. Sarah wanted to go downstairs to the little shanty and phone for the police, but Marlene couldn't let her go. Instead, they huddled in a corner of Sarah's room away from the window, staying close together. Sarah dozed a few times, but Marlene was still wide awake when the dawn broke, her heartstrings trembling like tightropes.

When the birds began to sing, Sarah sat up, blinking in the faint light of the dawn. She looked around, pushing a hand through her loose gray hair. It was strange to see it without her *kapp*.

"Come on, Marlene," she said. "He can't still be out there – if it was even Jeremy in the first place. Let's go downstairs and make breakfast."

"*Nee*," Marlene panted, terrified. "Let's wait until Zeb gets here."

"*Liebchen*, we're not going to let him see us in our nightclothes," said Sarah firmly. "It's all right. Come on."

Bolstered by Sarah's cheerful fearlessness, Marlene managed to go back to her room and struggle into her clothes. When she came into the kitchen, Sarah had already whipped her hair into shape and was standing by the table, industriously sweeping the bits of porcelain into a little heap.

"I'm so sorry about your table," said Marlene. The scratch was even worse in the daylight; the window gaped, and a cold wind blew through it.

"*Ach*, your *onkel* did much worse with a carving knife once," said Sarah dismissively. "It'll polish out, mostly. Get that dustpan for me, would you?"

Marlene fetched it from the cleaning cupboard and pushed the remnants of the salt and pepper pots into it with the brush. She dumped them into the garbage, feeling sick to her stomach. This time, they'd been the only victims of Jeremy's visit. But if he came again...

"I can't stay here, Sarah," she said.

Sarah turned, leaning on the broom, her expression sharp.

"Now what nonsense is that?" she said. "We've been over this."

"I know, but look what he's done," Marlene cried, gesturing around her.

"We don't know that it was Jeremy."

"Who else could it be, Sarah?" said Marlene. "We both know that it's him. And what if, next time, he comes here and hurts you?"

The old woman folded her arms. "I'm not going to let you go home so that he can hurt *you*, Marlene."

"Then I'll go somewhere else," said Marlene. "I'll go and find work in another town. But I'm not going to let Jeremy hurt you."

"It's no use to run, *liebchen*." Sarah sighed, her face relenting. "If he's found you here, he'll keep coming after you."

Marlene ran a hand over her face. "It was that letter to Mona," she said. "The postman must have recognized my handwriting. I didn't think to change it."

"If Jeremy will use those means to find you, he'll use anything. He'll come after you no matter where you go," said Sarah flatly. "It's no use running."

"Then what should I do, except to go home?"

"We'll call the police," said Sarah firmly. "If he wants to

behave like a rogue *Englischer*, then let the *Englischers* deal with him. That man deserves to be in jail."

Marlene sat down, abruptly feeling so miserable that her legs would no longer hold her. "What *gut* will that do?" she said. "I don't want to get *Englischers* involved. I just want to get away from here so that you can be safe, Sarah. I don't care about anything else. I just want you to be all right."

Sarah shook her head. "Going home is not an option. You're staying here."

"Sarah..." Marlene groaned.

"I'm much older than you, Marlene," said Sarah with a note of her usual cheerfulness. "I've had a lot more practice at winning disagreements."

Chapter Nine

Zeb frowned as he walked through the gate of Sarah's farmyard. It was a beautiful, crisp fall morning; the hawthorn bushes along the lane were glowing with berries, and the great old oak tree that spread its protective arms over the top of the farmhouse was decked out in the full splendor of its fall colors. There were birds singing everywhere, their melody summoning the holidays. In the tranquil setting, raised voices coming from the farmhouse were utterly out of place.

He quickened his step. He could definitely hear Marlene's voice now, and it didn't sound musical anymore; it sounded harsh and hysterical, the cry of a frightened animal rather than the speech of a human. Rounding the turn, he stepped into the farmyard, and his heart flipped over. The big front window of the kitchen was shattered. A round hole had been broken in the middle, shards of glass jutting all around the gap.

"Marlene?" Zeb rushed forward. "Sarah!" He crossed the farmyard in a series of long bounds, leaped up the porch steps, and yanked the kitchen door open.

Sarah and Marlene were facing one another over the kitchen table. There was an ugly scratch in it, but it was no uglier than the naked fear on both their faces. Sarah's arms were crossed, and Marlene slumped in a chair, her face pale. When she turned her gentle eyes on him, the light had left them. She looked crushed.

"Are you all right?" Zeb gasped.

"We're fine, Zeb," said Marlene. She looked away, but her voice was thick with tears.

"*Danke*." Sarah smiled at him. Her eyes were scared; the smile never reached them.

"What happened?" Zeb asked.

Sarah looked at Marlene, whose eyes were glued to the table. "Nothing," she said. "Don't worry about us. Please just go on with feeding the animals. I'll call you when breakfast is ready."

"It's not nothing, Marlene," said Sarah.

"Sarah, please." Marlene swallowed.

The silence was cold, awkward. Zeb resisted the urge to

intervene. All he wanted to do was to cross the floor, to scoop Marlene's slender body into his arms and cuddle her close where nothing could ever make her look so pale and afraid ever again. Instead, he looked over at the broken window.

"We'll go into town and get that repaired," said Sarah.

"I think I should board it up for you just for now," Zeb offered. "You'll be so cold in here in the meantime, and the wind might snuff out the gas stove." He backed away. "I'm going to fetch some boards from the barn."

As soon as the door closed behind him, Zeb could hear the argument starting again. His heart felt like it would explode. Now more than ever, he wished Marlene would tell him whatever the ugly secret was that had turned her so pale today – and what about it had caused that window to shatter. If she'd only trust him, he was sure he could help her. But even now, she wouldn't tell him. Was it any use trying to reason with her anymore?

The animals called to him, excited for their breakfast, when he stepped into the barn. He picked up some dusty boards, a hammer and nails, and headed back to the farmhouse. They were still arguing. Zeb's heart felt suddenly leaden. What had he done to let Marlene down? There were so many times that she looked at him as if she felt something of the spark that roared in his chest every time he laid eyes on her, and yet she kept him always, always, at arm's length. Perhaps it was time to accept the fact that she'd never let him in.

The shouting switched off abruptly when he came in again. "This won't take a minute," he said, trying his best to sound cheerful. He lifted one of the boards to the kitchen window, and as he turned, he spotted it. A brick. It lay on the kitchen floor, the scratch in the table marking its trajectory.

Zeb almost dropped the board. He spun around, horrified. "Someone threw a brick through your window in the night?" he cried. "Sarah, what happened?"

Sarah gave Marlene a defiant look. "It was…"

"Sarah," Marlene pleaded.

"I'm sorry, Marlene," said Sarah, "but if you won't let me call the police, at least let me tell Zebadiah."

Marlene looked at him again, and her eyes were two raw holes of pain, ripped in a face as gaunt as a skull. Fresh tears spilled onto her cheeks, and Zeb started nearer almost involuntarily. Oh, how much he wanted to hold her.

"Please," said Sarah.

Marlene buried her face in her hands. "All right," she groaned. "All right. Tell him. Everything, Sarah – every last thing. I can't bear to keep secrets anymore. I'm sorry, Zeb. I'm so, so sorry."

Zeb turned to Sarah. At last, he was about to hear Marlene's secret.

Chapter Ten

Marlene's entire body was trembling. She kept her face safely hidden in her hands as Sarah began to speak to Zeb, and with every word, she doubted more and more that she'd done the right thing. At worst, this would put Zeb in terrible danger.

And at best, it would drive him out of her life forever, the only man she knew she could trust in the whole world.

"Zeb, you'd better sit down," Sarah was saying.

Marlene couldn't look. She didn't want to see his face. She heard the scrape as he pulled out a chair and sat.

"We didn't tell you everything about Marlene," said Sarah.

There was a pause. Marlene couldn't bear to imagine what Zeb's face looked like; but when he spoke, his voice was like the rest of him. As steady as a stone wall. "It's all right. You don't have to tell me."

"I think we do. We need help," said Sarah. "Marlene was trying to get away from everything that's ever hurt her, but it followed her here."

Zeb said nothing.

"As you probably remember, since you went to school with her for a few years, Marlene's never really had a family," said Sarah. "Her *mudder* died in childbirth, leaving her an only child with her *vadder*. My *brudder* was a *wunderlich* man – not unlike you, in fact, Zeb – but he fell very ill when Marlene was about nine years old. He had no choice but to hire a nurse, a sharp woman who was mostly interested in slacking whenever she could. She mostly ignored poor little Marlene. Of course, none of us knew then. Marlene's *vadder* was being eaten up by that cancer, and Marlene just didn't know any different."

Zeb made a small noise in the back of his throat. A noise of empathy, Marlene guessed. He would soon lose that empathy, she thought, because the next part of the story was the part where she ruined everything.

"Well, once her *vadder* died, Marlene came to live with us," said Sarah. "We were delighted to have her, poor thing. She'd already been through so much, and I could never have children, you know. And in due course, she met a young man named Jeremy from Sunny Bay."

"That's some distance away," said Zeb.

"*Jah*, he was visiting family here for the summer when they met. It seemed to us, at first, like a love story. They seemed to fall in love so completely that none of us even wondered how it had happened so quickly. Marlene married him that fall; he was her first love."

There was absolutely no sound from Zeb. Marlene could almost feel him slipping away from her, feel the love in his eyes turn to hatred, just as it had done with Jeremy. *If* there had ever been love in him when he looked at her.

"That was five years ago," said Sarah. "Marlene was just eighteen when she married. In those five years, I only saw her twice − at her *onkel's* funeral, and one Thanksgiving. And both times I knew something was wrong, but it was only a few days ago that she told me what had been happening."

Marlene stiffened.

"Her husband has been hurting her," said Sarah softly. "Beating her."

There was a sharp breath from Zeb, as if someone had slapped him. Marlene knew he was appalled that she could be so pathetic, that she could so horrifically fail someone as she'd failed Jeremy.

The silence wore on. The cuckoo clock ticked. Outside, Muddy whinnied, wondering why he hadn't been fed yet.

"Did he throw the brick?" Zeb's voice was just the same as always: straight and sturdy as a country road.

"*Jah*," said Sarah. "We think so."

"Then you must be kept safe," said Zeb.

Marlene looked up. When her eyes met Zeb's, she could see deep sorrow in them, but also something she realized she never expected: love. It was a deep-running, far-reaching kind of love that she glimpsed there, something that stretched out like an ocean, and it took her breath away.

"If he'd do that," said Zeb calmly, pointing at the window, "who knows what else he could do."

"Exactly," said Marlene. "That's why I have to go."

"You're going nowhere, young lady," said Sarah.

"I have to," Marlene cried, the stress blazing in her voice. "I can't let anything happen to you!"

"Marlene."

She turned to Zeb. He had leaned forward in his chair, and he was so tall that the movement had brought him unexpectedly closer. Much closer. His fresh, country smell surrounded her, and he reached forward with one of his huge hands, placing it briefly over her arm. The touch was platonic, as it now had to be; but it stilled her.

"Stay here," said Zeb. "Don't be afraid. I'll keep you and your aunt safe. I promise."

"I can't," she whispered.

"Let me prove to you that you can," said Zeb. His eyes poured gentleness into her. "Give me three days. Just until the weekend. Let me show you that you'll be safe."

"Zeb," Marlene whispered. She couldn't say it out loud: that she was sorry he hadn't known. That he had to be aware, now, that there was no way they could be together, ever. Divorce could never happen. Marlene could hide from Jeremy all she liked; but in the eyes of the church, they were united until death did them part.

He smiled, and she knew he knew.

"Trust me," he said.

She wanted to. With every bone in her body, she wanted to, but she couldn't. His love could never defeat her fear. "Three days," she said. "Not an hour more."

Zeb nodded. Then he pushed back his chair and rose. "I'm going to feed the animals," he said. Without further ado, he turned and was gone.

Chapter Eleven

The steady, rhythmic thump of a hammer on wood was soothing somehow. Each blow brought satisfaction, knowing that he was one step closer to finishing his work. Stepping back, Zeb wiped sweat from his row. The fence boards that an unruly bull had broken that morning lay in the grass at his feet; new boards gleamed in the sunshine, the fence whole and restored once more. Zeb wished all of his problems could be so easily solved.

Marlene. He closed his eyes, patiently waiting for the wave of pain to wash over him. He could never again look at her in that way. He could never dream of being with her ever again, because no matter what that disgusting excuse for a human being − that Jeremy − had done to her, in the eyes of the church she would always belong to him.

But he could not tell himself not to fall in love with her. It was much, much too late for that.

As if summoned by his thoughts, when Zeb turned around, she had appeared on the flanks of the hill below him. He wasn't sure what he'd hoped when he'd come up to the high pasture to fix the fence; that she wouldn't come to find him, or that she would. He leaned on the fence, waiting, letting the midday sunshine bathe his shoulders in warmth.

She looked terrible. Underneath her *kapp*, her face was the color of window putty, deep circles sagging below her eyes. She'd wrapped her arms around herself as if for protection.

"Hello," he said, when she'd reached him and stood there for a few moments, too awkward to speak.

"Hi." Her voice was a worn-out husk of its usual self, as if she'd used it all up in crying.

Zeb wanted so much to wrap his arms around her. He shook himself, leashing his thoughts. No more of that. He was looking at another man's wife.

"Are you all right?" he asked.

She didn't answer him. "Lunch is ready."

"*Danke*." Zeb scooped up his hammer and tin of nails, the broken boards. "Perfect timing." He gave her his best smile, but she didn't return it.

Walking down the hill, he made sure to keep his strides short so that she could easily keep up. She was silent for a few minutes; the house had come into view, and Zeb's heart had begun to burst with fear that she'd never say anything, when she finally spoke.

"Zeb, I'm sorry."

Surprised, he stared at her. "What do you have to be sorry about?"

"Everything." Her voice grew thick with tears. "I should have told you everything."

"I saw what it took from you just to let your aunt tell me." Zeb kept his voice low, like he did when he was working with a frightened animal. It worked on them; he could only pray it would work on Marlene. "It was brave of you, Marlene. I understand why you didn't say anything until now."

A tear ran down her cheek. Zeb's heart felt ripped for her.

"*Danke*," she whispered. "I wish I could stay here. I really do. But I can't."

"Don't try to decide now," he said, smiling. "You've still got two and a half days." He paused. "I don't want you to feel trapped here, though."

"I don't," she almost shouted. When she glanced up at him, her eyes were filled with raw despair. "*Ach*, Zeb, I want nothing more than to be here. I love it here. I love it with..."

She didn't finish the sentence. "I just can't put my aunt in danger. Or you, for that matter."

"I'm fine, Marlene," said Zeb softly. "And she will be, too. We both want you to be here where we know you're safe. Where else would you go?"

"I don't know," Marlene admitted. Her voice grew pressured, slightly frantic, like a carthorse realizing its load is too heavy and scrambling to pull anyway. "I could go back home and tell the bishop everything, but I just know that he'd listen to Jeremy instead of me. And besides... even if he didn't, he'd tell me that..." She stopped.

"Tell you what?" Zeb coaxed.

"That I deserve this."

Marlene's voice felt like a kick in the belly. Zeb stopped, turning to face her. He'd never wanted so badly to touch her, but he kept his hands on the broken boards.

"Marlene, how could anyone deserve this?" he said.

"You don't understand." She wouldn't meet his eyes. "I do. That night that you took me to the hospital, I didn't have a bellyache. I lost..."

"I know," said Zeb. "Your *boppli* is in *Gott*'s hands, Marlene."

"Because of me."

"*Nee. Gott* called that child home to Him. You didn't do anything wrong."

She choked on her tears. "You don't understand."

"Maybe I don't understand, but I do understand a little of Him," said Zeb, "and I know that He knows what you've been through. He sees your pain, Marlene, and He would never reject you, no matter what's been done to you – or even your own mistakes."

She looked at him at last, and her eyes begged him to give her hope. "Are you sure?"

Zeb smiled. "I've never been so sure of anything in my life," he said.

It wasn't quite true. He was just as sure of one other thing: that he loved her, and that that love would have to burn forever and be forgotten.

Exhaustion had plunged Marlene into sleep that night after hours of staring at nothing. Her dreams were a crazed swirl, messy as her situation, senseless as her life so far: Jeremy at the altar; Jeremy with his belt in his hand, his eyes blazing like dry ice; Sarah screaming. Then Zeb, holding out his hand. *He would never reject you.* Perhaps it could be true, she thought in her dream. Perhaps it could, because Zeb hadn't rejected her, even after he knew the truth. If he had such grace, could

God's grace be even greater? She stepped toward him, but the floor opened under her feet and she fell, fell, fell. And always, always, there was a baby crying...

Marlene sat up. Sweat cooled on her skin, and she realized that she was shaking, but she wasn't sure why. The thing that was making her heart thunder wasn't fear. She closed her eyes, seeing Zeb in front of her again, feeling the rush of hope that the dream had sent through her. What if it really was true, and God would take her back despite it all? The thought made her veins fill with mercury.

"Lord, would You?" she whispered into the dark.

The question was much too intriguing to ignore. Marlene reached for the paraffin lamp on her nightstand and lit it, the warm flame rising solemnly in its glass shield, filling the room with a soft golden light that sparkled on the gold-leaf title of her Bible. She ran her fingers across the cover. Like everything else, Jeremy had used this Book as a weapon., tormenting her with verses that seemed to point out her continual failures. Could there be more to it than what he'd told her?

The look in Zeb's eyes had made her want to find out. She opened it at random, and the first verse that caught her eye was Romans 8:38. If even the heavenly angels, even death itself, could not separate her from the love of God, surely neither could her own mistakes?

That hope was just beginning to flame in her heart when she

heard it. A slamming noise, like a door closing outside. She sat bolt upright, the Bible sliding out of her lap, listening. Perhaps she was imagining things. It had sounded so much like a car door, but who would bring an *Englisch* car to an Amish farm in the middle of the night?

Then, footsteps. Marlene trembled. There was someone walking across the farmyard. The sound was soft, too soft to have woken her if she'd still been asleep, but she knew what it was. And she knew, abruptly, who it was that had just reached the porch; the footsteps sounded hollow on the wood.

Fear gripped her, but something in her roared louder. Sarah was right. The time for running was over. She had to do something else now, and she didn't know what it was, but it was time.

The front door hadn't opened, and Marlene knew that she had to move fast before he came into the house. Grabbing her flashlight, she blew out the lamp and hurried downstairs, holding the flashlight out in front of her like a shield. When she strode into the kitchen, his silhouette was sketched against the second, unbroken window, and it was him. There could be no doubt. She had dreaded his approach for so long, had loved it so well once, that she would know it anywhere.

Jeremy *was here.*

She quailed for a moment, hesitating, but the words she'd just read seemed to have burst into flame inside her. It was time to face him. She strode forward, kicked open the front door, and shouted his name.

"Jeremy!"

He was standing at the corner of the porch, looking through one of the kitchen windows. Turning, he staggered slightly, propped himself up against the wall of the house with one hand. His eyes were only half-focused, but the malice in them glittered unmistakably as they rested on Marlene. Her courage melted away like milk into sand. She could only stand there, staring at him, as he leered at her. His face was as loose and clumsy as his movements, stupid with drink.

"Marlene," he slurred. "Did you think you could run from me?" He took a fumbling step closer to her. "You're my wife."

"I know," said Marlene. She stepped back, out of his reach.

"Come on," he said, swaying a little. "Time to go home."

Marlene took the deepest breath she could.

"I'm not going home, Jeremy," she said softly.

He blinked at her. Defiance wasn't something that Jeremy was used to. "Don't be stupid, woman," he growled, steadying on his feet. "I said we're going home."

"*Nee.*" Marlene had never said that word to him before. It was bitter, but bitter like medicine, not poison. The effort of it took her breath away; she stared at him, speechless, trembling in every cell of her body, waiting for him to react.

His eyes darkened like thunderclouds. "I should have known you never loved me," he said. "You hate me, don't you? You've hated me since you married me. You were just looking for someone to pay all your bills. Five years I've worked my fingers to the bone for you, woman, and now you think you can walk away like some *Englischer!*"

His words thrust into her, sharp as blades. Marlene struggled to take a breath, forcing them back. "I don't hate you," she said softly.

"Then come home," growled Jeremy.

Hot tears were chasing each other down her cheeks. "*Nee,*" she whispered.

He lunged at her, and she didn't think she had the strength to run, and that was when the calm voice floated up toward them from the farmyard, quiet in the still night, yet final as a slamming door.

"Stop," it said.

Marlene turned.

The moonlight spilled richly over Zeb's shoulders, glowing in his soft eyes. He stood in the middle of the yard as straight as a pillar, his great arms folded; his muscles were tense against his jacket, but there was no hatred in his eyes.

"Don't take a step closer to her," he said.

"This ain't none of your business," Jeremy slurred, waving a dismissive hand at Zeb. "She's my wife."

"Your wife, but not your possession," said Zeb. He took a single step closer, claiming two feet of ground. "Get away from her."

Something in Jeremy's expression broke, and it grew as dark as dried blood, dark as the bruises that Marlene had hidden so well after every time that his face took on that depth of violence. "I see now," he snapped, spinning to face Marlene, suddenly agile. "You've run away with this fool like some common *Englisch* hussy!"

"*Nee!*" Marlene cried. "Jeremy, I would never—"

But Jeremy was done listening. He launched himself toward her, his hands reaching for her throat, and Marlene let out a cry of terror as she scrambled backwards. Her back met the porch railing, slamming into it, knocking the breath from her lungs as Jeremy's body crushed her against it. His fingers were clawing over her throat, her chest; the stale smell of old alcohol huffed in her face. She slammed her hands against his shoulders, and his hands found her throat.

"You'll regret everything you've done to me," he spat in her face. She tried to breathe, but only a tiny thread of air found its way to her lungs, and panic swamped her. This was how she was going to die...

There was a great thump beside her, shaking the porch floor, and Jeremy's hands were wrenched from her throat with a force that threw her to her knees. She heard Jeremy staggering backward, and then Zeb was standing over them.

"Jeremy," he was saying, his voice still level, but tight with exertion. "I'm not involved with your wife, but I'm not going to let you harm her."

Saliva was dripping from her bottom lip as she fought for breath. Wheezing, the taste of blood in her mouth, she looked up. Jeremy was standing a few feet away; he didn't seem hurt, but his eyes were wary. Zeb must have simply lifted him and dumped him on the other side of the porch. All Marlene could think about was that Zeb couldn't hit him. She couldn't let Zeb break the Amish way of nonresistance for her.

"Zeb, get away from here," she croaked. "Don't fight him. Please."

"I'm not going to fight anyone," said Zeb calmly. He was holding out both hands to Jeremy, palms out, placating. "I just want you to stop hurting Marlene."

"You can't tell me what to do with my wife," Jeremy snarled.

Marlene saw his eyes scan up and down Zeb's giant frame. She struggled to her feet. "Jeremy, please," she begged. "Please, let's just talk about this."

His shoulders relaxed slightly, but she could still see that the alcohol was gripping him, making his thoughts run wild.

"We'll talk about this when we get home. Stop being silly, Marlene. It's time to go. Now. Right now."

Marlene shook her head, the tears continuing to splash on her neck and chest. It took all the strength in the world for her to squeeze out the small word she wished she'd learned five years ago when he first asked her to marry him. "*Nee.*"

Jeremy let out a wordless growl of drunken rage. "Come, woman!" he snarled, and lunged forward. Zeb stepped between them, extending a great hand, placing it on Jeremy's chest with no pressure, but rock-solid strength.

"Stop," he said again.

"Or what?" Jeremy spat.

"I don't need to fight you to stop you," said Zeb simply.

"You're not going to stop me." Jeremy lurched forward, swinging his skinny fists.

Zeb dodged them both with the agility of a man who worked with animals, sidestepping, and Jeremy stumbled past, catching himself on the railing.

He turned, and Marlene screamed. "Jeremy, *nee!*"

He was already coming again – not at Zeb, but at Marlene – his head lowered, charging back up and at her like a bull to bring her to the ground the way he'd done so many times. Marlene let out a scream of fear. Before she could run, Zeb had seized Jeremy by the back of his shirt, yanking him back with effortless strength. Jeremy stumbled, landing heavily on his backside. The indignity turned him dangerous. He was back on his feet almost before he had fallen, and this time, he moved artfully.

Keeping his feet under him, he struck straight for Zeb's face with one fist. Zeb dodged, but Jeremy's second blow caught him in the stomach. When the big man doubled over, Jeremy lunged at him. Even then, one blow from Zeb could have sent him flying, but instead Zeb tried to get out of the way. He moved too slowly. Jeremy slammed his full weight into him, and he toppled like a falling redwood, landing on his back on the stairs - both of them tumbling one over the other down onto the dirt.

"Zeb!" Marlene shrieked. She ran after them both. They'd landed on the hard ground; and in the moonlight, blood gushed down the side of Zeb's face, and he moved very slowly. Jeremy was already scrambling to his feet. He turned, his eyes locking on Marlene, but Zeb was already trying to get up, and Jeremy was limping. He backed away, hobbling and swaying.

"This isn't over," he growled. "I'm coming for you."

He turned and fled into the dark, weaving and limping, and Marlene ran down the stairs to where Zeb was slowly sitting up. One side of his face was a mask of blood. "Are you all right?" she gasped.

"I'm fine," said Zeb, his voice as steady as ever as he raised a hand to the gash.

Another sound tore the night. The roar of an engine – a car engine. Marlene closed her eyes, wishing she could block out the sound.

It was just even more proof that the man she'd married had slipped even further away from her than she'd imagined.

Chapter Twelve

Zeb winced despite his best efforts as the nurse's gloved fingers explored the gash on the side of his face. "Sorry," she said. "This is quite a deep cut, Mr. Hartzler. You should have come in right when it happened, not waiting till morning."

"*Ach*, I didn't want to leave the farm in the dark," said Zeb. That much was true. He'd waited for dawn to break, and for Sarah and Marlene to be safely having breakfast, before leaving them. And even then, it was only because Sarah had insisted that he have the cut seen to at the local hospital.

"Well, I'm afraid you might be left with a scar," said the nurse, "but I'll still be able to glue it for you. It'll heal up just fine."

"I don't mind a scar," said Zeb. He clutched his straw hat on his knees.

"What happened?" the nurse asked, her tone conversational. She began to fill a syringe with clear liquid, and the glinting of the needle in the bright light made Zeb feel a little queasy. He smiled at her, hoping she'd keep talking to distract him. She was a comforting figure, just portly enough to be motherly, with streaks of gray in her frizzy black hair.

"I was protecting a friend from a man who wanted to hurt her," he said. "And we fell."

"Fell?" The nurse raised an eyebrow. "Mr. Hartzler, if you've been assaulted, you should speak to the police."

"That's up to my friend," said Zeb, unruffled. "She'll decide if she wants to involve them."

"She should," said the nurse.

"I think so, too. But it's up to her."

There was a tiny stab of pain above his ear, and he flinched a little.

"Sorry," the nurse said again. "It's just a bit of local anesthetic, so that you won't feel anything while I glue this."

"That's okay," said Zeb, trying to smile. She patted his shoulder. "Not a fan of needles?"

"Never have been."

"You'll be all right." A troubled look crossed the nurse's face. "Not everyone is so lucky."

"How do you mean?" asked Zeb, hoping to keep her talking so he didn't have to think about the strange tugging sensations at his cut.

"My paramedic friend was in here just a few hours ago with a young man who was involved in a horrible accident," said the nurse. "We tried to get him back, but his heart must have stopped on impact. It was a terrible accident, and the strangest thing – he was Amish like you, but it seemed like he was the driver."

Zeb felt his body grow cold all over. "A young man, you said?" he said, trying to keep his voice calm. "Skinny?"

The nurse drew back, her expression cautious. "Why?" she asked. "Do you think you might know him?"

"I can only think of one person in our community who would break our ways and drive a car," said Zeb quietly.

"I can't tell you any identifying details about a patient unless you're their next of kin," said the nurse. "Are you related to this person you think might be the victim?"

"*Nee*, but I know someone who is," said Zeb.

The nurse nodded. "Then they'll have to call the hospital and find out," she said. "There was no identification on him, obviously, since he was Amish. But we're still trying to figure out who he was, poor man. It would be helpful if you could ask your friend to call or stop in if they haven't seen their relative." Her expression softened. "I'm so sorry."

She went back to working on Zeb's cut, and his heart ached as he prayed. He didn't know whether or not to pray that the dead man would be Jeremy; but if it *was* him, he prayed that Marlene would somehow find a way to make peace with it.

Marlene was very quiet as she sat in the buggy on the drive back to Sarah's home from the hospital. She couldn't even think of what to pray, so she did nothing but offer up her feelings to God, mixed and wild though they were. Chief among them was simple gratitude that Jeremy's face hadn't been injured in the accident. When the nurse had gently pulled the sheet back from his head, his skin had been a terrible shade of white, but his eyes and mouth were closed, and the lines of rage and worry that had always creased his skin were gone. He looked as though he were asleep, even though Marlene had known that he wasn't. She'd just nodded once to the nurse and heard herself speaking as if it was someone else's voice: "Yes, that's him."

Now she sat beside Zeb, listening to the arthritic clop of old Muddy's hooves on the road, wondering what to feel. There was a part of her that grieved in a way. It was not longing, but it was a lack of balance somehow, as if she kept reaching out to steady herself on a solid object that had suddenly disappeared, leaving her stumbling. Jeremy's presence in her life had been a blight at times, but it had been a constant, and now it was over. She wished she could cry the tears that weighed on her heart.

"I don't understand," she said at last.

Zeb looked over at her. His eyes were flooded with sorrow, and he said nothing, but his silence invited her to speak.

"I don't understand what could have happened to Jeremy," said Marlene. "What made him become the way that he was?" She stared at him. "Why would he be like that? If he hadn't turned from our ways, he'd still be alive now. Surely, he must have known that what he was doing was wrong."

"I wish I could make sense of this for you," said Zeb quietly.

"So do I. I just want to understand what he was thinking," said Marlene. "Where did he get that car? Why would he decide..." She shook her head. "*Ach*, Zeb, maybe if I had loved him better..."

For the first time, Zeb interrupted her. "None of this is your fault," he said, his voice calm and sure. "No matter what happens, no one is responsible for another person's choices."

She wanted so much to believe him. Maybe she could.

"I'll have to go back home now," she said. "For the funeral."

Zeb nodded. She watched him closely, but his face was blank, wiped clean of emotion. "I'll drive you to the bus stop," he said.

Marlene let a few beats of silence pass between them before speaking. "*Danke*, Zeb," she said. And she didn't just mean for driving her.

Chapter Thirteen

Almost no one came to the funeral. Just Mona, who stood with her, and Jeremy's family, who did not. The bishop kept it short. It occurred to Marlene that perhaps he didn't know what to say about a man who would have been shunned if he had survived.

She didn't know either. Wrapped in her black mourning, standing close beside Mona (who did not shed a single tear), Marlene watched as Jeremy's brothers lowered his handmade coffin into the grave they'd dug the night before. It was a slight jolt as she realized that she'd looked at him for the last time. She'd never see those blue-gray eyes staring at her again.

She cried a little then, for everything that her girlish heart had longed for five years ago when she first became a bride. Then Mona put an arm around her shoulders, and they walked away, and left Jeremy's body in the cold dirt where it belonged, and Marlene knew that she was never going to visit his grave.

~

Dear Marlene,

I don't mean to intrude with this letter, so please don't feel that you have to respond right away.

I pray that all is well with you, and that Gott *has given you peace in your heart in this difficult time. I just wanted to let you know that you're in my prayers every day, and in Sarah's, of course. Everything is fine on the farm, although the winter has been a little unkind to Muddy's old bones, but Sarah's vet is giving him something that makes him almost as frisky as a foal again. The windowpane is all fixed up and Sarah is safe and warm in her* haus.

I pray you are well and that you see the love and power of the Lord's hand in your life in the days that lie ahead. My prayers go with you.

Sincerely,

Zeb Hartzler

Marlene sighed as she reached the end of the letter she'd read a thousand times. She stroked the worn paper with her thumb, watching it slightly smudge the name that had been meticulously signed at the bottom of the page. For such a hulking man, Zeb had strangely fussy, tidy handwriting. She wondered why he'd felt the need to sign the letter with his last name. Did he think that she would have forgotten who he was?

She gazed out of the window at the snowbound landscape, feeling Christmas in the air. It would be the first time that she spent it completely alone in the big house she'd once shared with Jeremy. It felt strange – unburdened, somehow. There would be no shouting and expectations for her to have the house looking perfect for Jeremy's family to arrive. There would be no more bruises underneath her clothes or quiet tears in the bathroom in the dead of night.

She wrapped her arms around herself and stepped outside into the garden, gazing at nothing. The sale of the animals and farm equipment had been enough to buy her some time and to buy her the supplies to start baking small things that she sold at the *Englisch* bakery in town; none of the Amish bakeries were interested in working with her. It was comfortable enough, she supposed. She was not shunned. She could go to church and sit at the end of one of the benches at the post-church meal, and people would even smile at her sometimes. It was peaceful enough.

It just felt so empty. As if her heart had been hollowed out, all the pain and bitterness and fear scooped out and thrown away, leaving an empty shell that waited and waited for something to fill it.

She was still gazing at the back garden when a merry voice called from the front door. "Oh, Marleeene! I've brought soup!"

Marlene turned, stepping back into the kitchen and closing the door behind her. "Mona," she said, smiling freely. "What a nice surprise."

"Well, I couldn't leave you to mope around all day," said Mona briskly, shaking the snow from her shoulders as she set a still-steaming pot of soup in a knitted cozy down on the stove. "*Mamm* and *Daed* said it would be all right if I brought you this. It must be tiring, cooking just for one all the time."

"Better than cooking for two used to be," said Marlene. She lifted the lid. "Mmm, chicken noodle. You know just what I like."

"Of course, I do," said Mona. "I'm your best friend." She looked down at the letter on the kitchen table, then raised an eyebrow to Marlene. "Have you written back to him yet?"

"*Nee.*" Marlene sighed, trailing her fingers over the beloved page.

"Marlene." Mona shook her head. "Why not?"

"He won't take offense."

"I know he won't. That's entirely beside the point," said Mona.

"Well, what is the point, then?"

"*Marlene*." Mona put everything down, came around the table to face her, and gripped both of Marlene's shoulders in her hands. "Look at me."

Startled, Marlene met Mona's eyes. They sparkled, but they were dead serious.

"It's been three months since that disgusting beast of a man died," said Mona.

"Mona!"

"I'm not taking it back," said Mona sharply. "But that's not the point. Three months, Marlene. He's dead and gone, and for three long months, you've been moping around this house staring at nothing, all by yourself – when there's a man waiting for you back in Baker's Corner who loves you."

"I don't know," said Marlene. "I don't think it's a *gut* idea..."

"Oh, so you think it's a *gut* idea to sit here alone?" said Mona. "Failing to grieve for the man who never loved you? And it's not a *gut* idea to get the first bus to Baker's Corner and run back to that farm and run back to that man who stood up for you, the man who comforted you, the man who has respected you in friendship a thousand times more than Jeremy ever respected you in marriage?"

The passion in her voice struck deep into the very center of Marlene's heart. She stared at her.

"Marlene," said Mona, more softly, this time. "It was a terrible thing that you've suffered, but *Gott* used it mightily to show you His love. But you're free from it now, my friend, or you could be, if only you chose it. The cage door is wide open. You just need to walk out of it. Take the gift of grace that *Gott* is holding out to you and leave your old life behind."

Tears stung Marlene's eyes. "Mona," she whispered, "I think I've been a fool."

Mona grinned. "And what are you going to do about it?"

Marlene's heart was racing, feeling like it was filling every inch of her body with a pounding joy and wonder, a thrill that coursed through her as if she'd just jumped into the great expanse of sky and discovered against all the odds that she had wings.

"I'm going to sell it," said Marlene. She wasn't sure if she was crying or laughing or both, but it felt good. "I'm going to sell everything and leave it all behind."

Mona hugged her so tightly she thought her lungs might burst. "Be free, Marlene."

Marlene closed her eyes, returning her friend's embrace.

"I am free," she whispered.

No one was at the bus stop to meet Marlene when she got there. Of course not; no one here knew that, in the last two weeks, she'd sold Jeremy's farm, bought a bus ticket, and come to Baker's Corner with nothing but that same small canvas bag. She'd even given all her old clothes to Mona. She was determined to bring nothing with her into her new life.

She didn't mind the walk, though. It was a perfectly sunny winter day, and her favorite gray dress – the one that Jeremy had always hated – was warm. She walked easily, enjoying the chirps of the surprised robins who came out to feel the sun on their feathers, feeling whole and yet empty. She prayed that she'd done the right thing, but her heart felt good.

Everything felt like mercy these days, everything tasted of love: the cascade of sunlight that poured over her, the crunch of the snow under her feet, the spreading beauty of the endless hills turned into a patchwork pattern by the walls and fences that slowly climbed their leisurely flanks. She breathed every moment of it, relishing all the little things. It felt like she'd been wrapped in a shroud for five years, unable to notice them, but now that she was free, every detail seemed magical.

Even walking unhurriedly, it was just over an hour and her legs had just begun to feel pleasantly tired when Marlene saw the row of snow-dusted hawthorn bushes and knew that she'd reached Sarah's farm. She slowed for a moment before turning into the yard, feeling a pang of nervousness. What if....

Nee. She shook her head firmly. She was finished with living with what-if, because she already knew the answer to that question: regardless of what happened, God would still love her. It was all that she needed. She had survived so much worse than any scenario she could imagine now. She strode into the farmyard with her head held high.

He was there.

Walking across the yard with his long, slow steps, a pitchfork in his hands, heaving a great pile of hay over Muddy's stable door and into the hay rack. The old horse ignored it, tipping his ears toward her and letting out a whinny of recognition. It made Zeb turn, lowering the pitchfork. His eyes were as serene as ever, but when they rested upon her, they widened in startled joy.

If she had been eighteen years old, and if she had loved Zeb the way that she had loved Jeremy, Marlene might have run to him. She might have called out his name in joy and flown across the space between them and flung her arms around his neck. She might have pressed herself against him and kissed him and done everything to show him how wildly her heart beat for him. But she did not love him the way that she loved Jeremy. What she felt now was different, and it was slower, and it was rich and it was steady and it was good and it was forever. Instead of speeding up, her heart seemed to slow in her chest when she laid eyes on him.

Zeb didn't move. He stood waiting, and she let the bag fall out of her fingers and walked across the yard without any hurry because there was none. There was a new scar above his eye, but it had healed well, even though the mark would be there forever. Marlene reached him and looked into his eyes, knowing at once that there was nothing she had to say. Her return said it all.

Even then, even so close to him and his fresh country smell, she didn't throw her arms around him. Instead, she just reached out and touched her fingertips to his palm.

"Hello," he said. His voice drizzled over her like warm honey.

She didn't proclaim her undying love. She just said, "Hello, Zeb."

But it was more than enough.

The End

Continue Reading...

Thank you for reading **Amish Escape. Are you wondering what to read next?** Why not read **Sally's Beau?** Here's a peek for you:

Am I destined to be an old maidel, Sally Wagler wondered not for the first time as she walked along the main road through the small town of Baker's Corner, Indiana.

The street was lined with shops and businesses, including the Wyses' bakery, as well as the dry goods store, a café, a furniture shop, and the feed store, which were all owned by local Amish families in the community.

The door of the bakery opened, and Sally's gaze was drawn to the young woman exiting. Her arm was linked with a handsome dark-haired man, and her dark green dress draped over her distended middle. Lovina Slagel and her husband,

Jeremy, had wed last summer, and their first child was due to arrive in less than two months.

A horse and buggy passed Sally on the road, and her attention shifted to the couple sitting close together on the bench seat. Nancy Springer and Will Helmuth would be married right soon and were looking forward to starting their life together.

Sally couldn't help feeling envious of them and their good fortune, with their happy future ahead of them. And the Slagels, too, with a new baby on the way. No matter that her conscience pricked her for harboring such an unbecoming emotion.

It was the first mild day after weeks of freezing temperatures and snowstorms that had kept most of the residents shut indoors, and it seemed as though the whole of Baker's Corner was out and about today, taking advantage of the break in the weather.

Yet despite the sun shining overhead, Sally's thoughts remained gloomy. Would she ever know the joy of a husband and children of her own?

It was hard not to feel disheartened when it seemed as though everywhere she looked, she was confronted by girls five or six years younger than she who were courting and planning their weddings—or already married and awaiting the arrival of a child. And yet, Sally didn't even have the prospect of a beau on the horizon.

There *had* been a boy many years ago. They had courted for a few months, and she'd been happily envisioning her future with him. But then the courtship had ended abruptly when he decided to move to another community and had not asked Sally to go with him.

She had been heartbroken by his defection, but later realized that it was the loss of her dream of a family that she mourned more than the absence of the boy himself. This had only proven that he wasn't the one meant for her.

VISIT HERE To Read More:

http://www.ticahousepublishing.com/amish-miller.html

Thank you for Reading

If you **love Amish Romance, Visit Here**

https://amish.subscribemenow.com/

to find out about all **New Hannah Miller Amish Romance Releases! We will let you know as soon as they become available!**

If you enjoyed ***Amish Escape,*** would you kindly take a couple minutes to leave a positive review on Amazon? It only takes a moment, and positive reviews truly make a difference. I would be so grateful! Thank you!

Turn the page to discover more Hannah Miller Amish Romances just for you!

More Amish Romance from Hannah Miller

Visit HERE for Hannah Miller's Amish Romance

https://ticahousepublishing.com/amish-miller.html

About the Author

Hannah Miller has been writing Amish Romance for the past seven years. Long intrigued by the Amish way of life, Hannah has traveled the United States, visiting different Amish communities. She treasures her Amish friends and enjoys visiting with them. Hannah makes her home in Indiana, along with her husband, Robert. Together, they have three children and seven grandchildren. Hannah loves to ride bikes in the sunshine. And if it's warm enough for a picnic, you'll find her under the nearest tree!

CPSIA information can be obtained
at www.ICGtesting.com
Printed in the USA
BVHW041834270122
627396BV00013B/557

9 798636 029335